Charles Robb

The New Sugar Canes

SALZWASSER VERLAG

Charles Robb

The New Sugar Canes

Reprint of the original, first published in 1859.

1st Edition 2022 | ISBN: 978-3-37512-176-1

Verlag (Publisher): Salzwasser Verlag GmbH, Zeilweg 44, 60439 Frankfurt, Deutschland
Vertretungsberechtigt (Authorized to represent): E. Roepke, Zeilweg 44, 60439 Frankfurt, Deutschland
Druck (Print): Books on Demand GmbH, In de Tarpen 42, 22848 Norderstedt, Deutschland

THE

NEW SUGAR CANES.

---◆---

AN INQUIRY INTO THE

NATURE, USES AND ECONOMIC VALUE

OF THE

Chinese and African Sugar Plants,

WITH SPECIAL REFERENCE TO WESTERN CANADA.

READ BEFORE

THE HAMILTON ASSOCIATION,

APRIL 18, 1859,

BY CHARLES ROBB, C. E.

PUBLISHED BY REQUEST.

HAMILTON :

BROWN & GREIG, JAMES STREET.

1859.

VERTICAL THREE ROLLER SUGAR MILL, FOR PRESSING CHINESE CANE

THE NEW SUGAR CANES.

The consideration of the subject to which I shall have the honor, on the present occasion, of directing the attention of the Association, has been suggested to me by my esteemed friend Mr. Adam Brown, who, on a recent visit to New York, procured a copy of a work by Mr. Henry S. Olcott,* an eminent Agriculturist of New York State, embodying the fullest, most recent, and authentic information on the subject. Being strongly impressed with the opinion that the introduction of this new branch of Agricultural Industry into Canada on a scale commensurate with its importance, would be of signal benefit to the Province under its present circumstances, Mr. Brown did me the honor of requesting me to investigate the subject in detail, with the view of bringing it under the notice of farmers throughout the country, in the event of the result of the inquiry proving satisfactory. I have, with the consent of the Council, taken the liberty of laying my observations, in the first instance, before the Society, hoping thereby at once to elicit some further valuable information on the subject, and to obtain the benefit of your verdict as to the propriety of directing public attention it.

This is by no means the first time, as you are all probably aware, that these interesting Plants have been brought under notice in this Province. For upwards of five years they have been cultivated with more or less success in the neighbouring States, chiefly, however, in an experimental manner, and on a small scale ; and during last year, patches of the Sorgho, or Chinese Sugar Cane, were grown by some enterprising farmers in this neighbourhood with fair success and encouraging results, considering the rudeness of the apparatus employed, and the general want of information on the subject. The inducements to continued and extended

---

* *Sorgho and Imphee ; the Chinese and African Sugar Cane. A Treatise upon their Origin, Varieties and Culture. By Henry S. Olcott. New York: A. O. Moore, 140 Fulton Street, 1858.*

operations are at the present time vastly more powerful than ever before in the history of the Province. Circumstances seem to conspire to point to this enterprise as an important means of retrieving somewhat of our national prosperity. The con'inued and most disheartening failures, during the past two successive years, in our wheat crops, to whatever cause this may be attributable—the increasing demand for Sugar, Molasses and Syrups, now no longer to be regarded as luxuries, but absolute necessaries of life—the rapid and alarming decline in the yield of Sugar in the West Indies, Brazils and the Southern States, and consequent rise in the prices—the expediency, (rendered but too manifest by the commercial crisis through which we are now passing), of restricting to the utmost the drain of money from the Province—and last, and most powerful of all, the operation of our new Tariff in virtually shutting us out from our accustomed markets in New York and Boston. Such a com· bination of circumstances cannot fail to secure a hearty welcome and a fair trial to a Sugar-bearing Plant, which appears capable of immediate acclimation in Canada, and promises, even were it only partially, to afford a supply within ourselves.

During the present year, in anticipation of the enhanced price of Sugar, the farmers in all parts of the country are devoting an increased amount of attention to the manufacture of Maple Sugar, but this product must obviously be available to a very limited extent as a substitute for the article to which we are accustomed. In various parts of the country, chiefly in the counties of Norfolk and Lincoln, farmers are already this season preparing to cultivate the Chinese Sugar Cane. But it is to be feared that, from want of proper information—from forming too sanguine anticipations—and from omitting the requisite precautions both in cultivating and applying the products, much disappointment may ensue, and a corresponding delay in the general introduction of these most useful plants.

The success of the Chinese Sugar Cane in the neighbouring States, both as respects its capability of cultivation and of yielding crystalized Sugar, is no longer a matter of doubt; and my object in the present Essay is to prove that the climate and soil of Western Canada are equally well adapted for the growth of such plants—to explain the most approved modes of culture, and the treatment after harvesting—to point out the various uses to which they may be applied—and finally to illustrate the economy and advantage which will result from their general introduction on a large scale into this country. For the practical instructions embodied in the Essay, I am mainly indebted to the work of Mr. Olcott, already referred to.

THE SORGHO, OR CHINESE SUGAR CANE.

Of the two varieties of Sugar-bearing Plants now under review, and called respectively the *Sorgho* and *Imphee*, or Chinese and African Sugar Canes, I give the precedence, on this occasion, to the former; not that its superiority in circumstances such as ours, has been clearly established, but because, having been for a longer period and more extensively tested in the neighbouring States, we can speak more positively as to its merits. Under this head, therefore, it should be distinctly understood that my remarks are applicable only to the Chinese variety, reserving the consideration of the African plants till the sequel.

HISTORY.

The name *Sorgho*, or *Sorgho Sucre*, as it is called in France and Algeria, where it has been pretty extensively cultivated, is believed by some authorities to be incorrect; but I consider it safest to adhere to the generic name SORGHUM, which is recognized as the legitimate one by Dr. Gray, in his "Manual of the Botany of the Northern United States."

It was introduced into America from France in 1854, by Mr. D. Jay Browne, of the United States Patent Office; from which, in accordance with the admirable system pursued in that Institution, packages of the seed were distributed to some of the more enterprising farmers and men of science in various parts of the Union. In spite of the feeling of suspicion with which all new projects are apt to be met, the success which attended these trials was so marked and so encouraging as at once to give rise to the demand for seed upon an extensive scale; but although the juice has been turned to profitable account in the manufacture of syrup for several years past, it was not until the beginning of last year that its complete success, as a source of crystalized sugar, was demonstrated in the detailed account of his experiments and observations, presented to the United States Agricultural Society by Mr. Joseph S. Lovering, a practical Sugar Refiner, as well as Agriculturist, in Pennsylvania.

APPEARANCE.

This Plant presents much of the appearance of Maize, or Indian Corn; and I may state here that the same analogy holds, in a general way, with respect to the mode of cultivation, the soil and climate required, and the seasons of growth and maturity. The *Sorgho* is, however, much more graceful in appearance than the Indian Corn, growing to an average height of about eleven feet, and each stalk being surmounted by an elegant tuft, forming the panicle or seed head; and, unlike the Maize, this is the only fruit produced by the plant. As it approaches maturity, the seeds undergo progressive changes in color and density, passing from green to violet, brown, and finally to a deep purple, almost black ; at which latter stage, and when the seed has become quite hard, the plant is ripe, and will yield its greatest amount of sugar. The stalks rarely grow single, but in groups, issuing from the same seed, forming a large stool, and occupying a considerable space. The general thickness of the stalk, when ripe, is about one and a quarter inch at one foot from the ground.

ADAPTATION TO CLIMATE.

In the systematic treatment of the subject, Climate is the first essential element which claims to be considered; and the method which I propose to adopt is, not to enter into any abstract or theoretical enquiry on this head, but simply to state the results of experience in climates similar to our own. From long habits of association, we are accustomed to regard sugar as the product of tropical and juxta-tropical regions ; and it is an undoubted fact that the plants which yield this precious commodity most luxuriantly and abundantly flourish best in proportion as they are grown nearer to the Equator. But waiving in the meantime all such considerations, I shall proceed to shew that this plant is capable of being successfully cultivated in Western Canada; reserving the results for the concluding part of my Essay.

Mr. Hind, in his admirable " Comparative view of the Climate of Western Canada," has expressed the opinion that all those portions of the Province lying south of the 44th parallel of latitude, enjoy a climate superior to those parts of the United States which lie to the north of the 41st parallel ; the latter comprising the whole of the New England States, together with the whole of New York, Michigan, Wisconsin and Iowa, and the Northern half of Pennsylvania, Ohio and Indiana. Mr. Hind's enquiries were made with special reference to the agricultural capabilities of the Province, and embraced all the considerations which these involve ; such as—adaptation to the growth of certain cereals—uniformity of distribution of rain over the agricultural months—humidity of atmosphere—comparative immunity from spring frosts and from summer drouths—and the favorable distribution of clear and cloudy days. These are all important elements in the question ; but in so far as our present enquiry is concerned, the most important of all, and that which chiefly regulates the growth of such crops, is the mean temperature of the summer months. This, so far from being over-rated, is, I believe, rather under-estimated by Mr. Hind. From our worthy Secretary, Dr. Craigie's Meteorological Observations, extending over a period of upwards of twelve years from the present, I find that the mean temperature at this place of the three hottest months of summer is 69.29°, whereas it is stated by Mr. Hind at only 66.54°* The year (1855) in which this mean temperature was lowest, was not more than two and a half degrees below the average.

For the sake of comparison, I have compiled a Table of the Mean Temperatures of the months of June, July and August; and also, of the Mean Temperatures throughout the year, at various points on the Continent, from 44° to 32° North Latitude inclusive.

Table of Mean Temperatures at various Latitudes.

PLACES.	LATITUDES.	MEAN TEMP. OF HOT MONTHS.	MEAN TEMP. OF WHOLE YEAR.
	°	°	°
Maine...............	44	67.71	45.3
HAMILTON......	43½	69.29	48.5
Wisconsin.........	43½	69.5	46.5
Massachusetts.......	42½	68.1	47.0
Providence, R. I.....	42	69.1	49.0
New York City.....	40½	71.6	52.0
New Jersey.........	40	72.43	52.0
Pennsylvania.......	39½	72.17	52.0
Kentucky..........	38	71.6	53.8
North Carolina......	35½	73.3	60.4
South Carolina......	34	78.5	62.0
Arkansas..........	33½	79.0	64.0
Georgia & Mississippi	32	80.0	67.0

From the above Table we perceive a remarkable regularity in the increase of temperature of the summer months in proportion as we approach the Line; but at 43.3°, the latitude of Hamilton, we find that we enjoy the same summer heat as at 41°, a point between Providence, R. I. and New York City.

With this and other well known advantages to compensate for our more northerly latitudes, and which are due, no doubt, mainly to our proximity to the Great Lakes, we are enabled to compete successfully, in point of climate, with all those States of the Union which I have enumerated.

I find from a Table printed in Mr. Olcott's interesting work, that records have been preserved of not less than 48 experimental crops of the Chinese Sugar Cane, raised during the year 1857 within the area referred

* Possibly this discrepancy may arise from the fact that Mr. Hind's observations were made at Toronto, and those of Dr. Craigie at Hamilton. The latter city, indeed, is popularly regarded as being hotter than the former.

to, and that of these the great proportion reached maturity, and were cut down in good condition, although some failed; no doubt, owing to the very unfavorable season, the mean temperature of the whole year being 3°, and that of the summer months 2° below average—the rains during these months being unusually protracted and severe—and the frosts having set in unusually early. Even in the State of Maine, the most northerly and most unfavorably situated of all, the experiment was successful. These facts set at rest the question as to the adaptation of our Climate to the growth of the plant, and it is unnecessary that I should say a word more on this part of the subject.

SOIL AND MANURES.

It is equally unnecessary to dwell upon the subject of Soil, for it is well known that the soils of Western Canada are unsurpassable for the growth of all kinds of cereals. With reference to the Sorgho, however, all accounts agree in giving the preference to soils which contain a considerable proportion of carbonate of lime, and where this is naturally deficient, frequent liming is recommended. But in this respect the soils of the Western Province are most specially adapted to the growth of this plant. As I had the honor of pointing out to the Society on a former occasion, the sub-soil clays overlying the Niagara Limestones, embracing the area comprehended between the Niagara and Grand Rivers, contain not less than 15 per cent. of carbonate of lime, while those in the neighbourhood of London, (and which may be taken as an exponent of the constituent elements of the clays of the whole Western District) contain nearly 30 per cent. On the other hand, the soils of the more easterly portion of the country are preferable, as being warmer, dryer and lighter, and less heavily charged with vegetable detritus, which, however favorable to the luxuriant growth of the plants, is deleterious in so far as the production of sugar is concerned.

The description given by Mr. Hunt of the soils covering the uplands on the East side of the Grand River, from Galt downwards for about 20 miles, approaches most nearly to that which has been found most favorable for the growth of these plants. With careful cultivation they will most probably succeed on all our soils, but where a choice is to be had, land of a medium quality, between a black loam and a pure sand or gravel, calcareous, and of moderate richness, is to be preferred. Good drainage is, of course, indispensible; and where means of artificial irrigation can be obtained, it will be found advantageous in the early stages of growth.

A

In the preparation of the soil for this crop, when intended for sugar making, animal manures, and all such as abound in ammonia, should be avoided, or very sparingly applied, as although these tend to the formation of a large luxuriant plant, the juice which it yields under such circumstances is so mucilaginous and saline as to render it extremely unsuitable for sugar making. As I have before stated that rich soil is not requisite, the land will probably be found to be sufficiently manured by ploughing in clover or other green crops or stubble. Should further manuring be required, ashes and bones would probably be found the best, and as sulphuric acid enters largely into the composition of the stalks, gypsum will be highly beneficial. After a crop of the sugar cane has been taken off, the *begasse*, or crushed canes, should invariably be returned to the field and ploughed under, provided the same field is to be used for the same crop in the succeeding season. The land should of course be well worked and deeply stirred both before sowing, and in the earlier stages of growth ; as it is essentially requisite that the progress of the plant to maturity should be stimulated to the utmost, which is best effected by the free access of the atmospheric influences to the parent seed and the roots. Notwithstanding the great size to which the plants grow, it is not an exhausting crop because the parts which are employed in manufacture consist only of carbonaceous matters, while the nitrogenized matters in the stalk and leaves are, or should be, returned to the soil.

CULTIVATION.

Having procured seed which can be relied on as genuine, it should be soaked before planting for twenty-four hours or even longer, in tepid water to which is added a small quantity of saltpetre, say about one ounce to six gallons of water: Previous to sowing (which should be done about the middle of May, or even a little later) it should be rolled in plaster. This treatment will expedite the germination of the seed by four or five days. About eight pounds of seed will be required per acre.

The seeds, when intended for sugar making, should be planted in drills (*not in hills*), about three feet six inches apart, and the plants in the row thinned out to eight or ten inches apart. An excellent plan for at once marking out the rows and preparing the ground for the immediate reception of the seed, is to use a small *one-horse* subsoil plough, thus thoroughly loosening the soil directly under the row of plants. The seeds when planted should be covered very loosely and lightly, as otherwise, should continued wet weather supervene, they will most certainly rot. A

B

moderate degree of moisture in the ground at the time of sowing is however advantageous. As soon as the rows can be seen—and this will be facilitated by dropping a radish seed at intervals in sowing—the cultivator or horse-hoe should be run through the piece to destroy the weeds while young, a man following with the hand hoe as in the case of Indian Corn. As soon as possible thereafter the one horse subsoil plough should be passed twice between each contiguous pair of rows, going up alongside one row and down by the other. This operation should be repeated at least once in the course of the season.

In about eight or ten days after sowing (unless rains intervene) the plants will become visible. The Sorgho is a very slow grower in its earlier stages, and for this reason will be very apt to discourage persons experimenting with it for the first time. In about a month, however, it will begin to shoot upwards with great rapidity, throwing out suckers which should be removed when the plants are about eighteen inches high, and developing long and graceful drooping leaves at each of the internodes on alternate sides of the stalks. About the middle of September the panicle, or seed-head, will be formed, and in about a month or five weeks thereafter, the crop will have reached maturity, as indicated by the color and hardness of the seeds, already adverted to. Neither leaves nor seeds should be removed from the stalks until ripe. Frosts do not appear to affect injuriously the yield of sugar, but rather the reverse; but warm Indian Summer weather coming after frost has a very marked injurious effect, both as respects quantity and quality. Consequently the period of cutting may be deferred until the middle of October, the usual period of Indian Summer, or it may take place at any convenient season between the time of ripening and the reaction of the weather, should any occur. I mention this to shew that a little latitude may be allowed in the time of cutting in order to suit the convenience of individuals in regard to the subsequent process, but it should be borne in mind that there is a culminating point in the development of the sugar which experience alone can determine. But even if it should be inconvenient to proceed with the extraction of the juice immediately after the plants reach maturity, they may, *if fully ripe*, be cut and housed or stacked in the field for a considerable time without sustaining any damage, provided rainy weather does not ensue. On no account should the crop, if destined either for the production of sugar or syrup, be cut down before it is perfectly ripe, nor should the juice be extracted until the subsequent processes can be carried on continuously and without delay, as in either case fermentation will immediately ensue, and the crop will be utterly ruined.

HARVESTING.

When the proper time arrives the leaves are first stripped as far as the joints extend, the seed-heads, with from eighteen inches to two feet of the top of the stalks, are then detached, and finally, the canes are cut off close to the roots with a corn-cutter, a large carving knife, or small sharp hatchet; then cut each cane into two parts, separating the eight lower joints from the upper ones, which contain but little sugar, but will make good syrup or molasses. Pile each sort into separate bundles, to be hauled to the press as soon thereafter as convenient. If necessary to keep them for some time before crushing, do not divide the stalks. The leaves may be cured and preserved as fodder, of which I shall say more hereafter, and the seed-heads should be made up into bundles and stored for future use as seed, if the crop proves to be of good quality.

CRUSHING THE CANES.

The next important step in the process is the extraction of the juice, and as, at this early stage in the history of this interesting branch of manufacturing industry, it is impossible, or at least does not form part of my present plan, to speculate upon the most economical method of disposing of the crop, I shall take it for granted that the farmer will undertake to make his own supply of sugar or syrup. It should here be remarked, however, that the results of operations on such a limited scale, and with such rude apparatus as individual farmers will probably be able to command, can scarcely be taken as a fair criterion of what might be done with a perfect system and perfect machinery, such as would be applied in the event of the manufacture being carried on upon a large scale.

For present purposes, then, I shall suppose that a portable sugar mill which would cost probably from $100 to $150 will be procured, either by the farmers in any particular locality clubbing together to defray the cost conjointly or otherwise, as may be found most convenient. Let no one who has taken the trouble to cultivate even a small crop of the Sorgho entertain the idea of making shift with wooden rollers, or any but a tolerable efficient crushing apparatus. For small operations, such as a breadth of half an acre or less, a hand-mill with iron rollers might suffice. Where steam or water power is not at command, a vertical Three Roller Sugar Mill with iron rollers and framing, and worked by two horses, and with a simple apparatus to guide the canes horizontally in passing between the rollers will, in my opinion, prove the simplest and most efficient form for this mode of working. (*See Frontispiece.*) Such a mill could be set up in working order by two men in a day. The rollers should be arranged so as, for the first squeeze, to be one-eighth of an inch apart, and for the second to touch each other; and thus very little of the juice will remain in the cane after leaving the mill. If time will admit, however, it will be prudent to pass the canes through the mill twice. The juice is received into a large vessel set immediately underneath the rollers, and should be subjected to the further treatment without an hour's delay.

The remaining steps, as well as the rationale of the process, are so fully, clearly and concisely described by Mr. Lovering, one of the most successful and intelligent operators hitherto, that I cannot do better than quote it entire, and recommend it to the careful attention of all who are interested in the subject :—

GENERAL PRINCIPLES.

The juice of the ripe Sorgho is composed of

1. Crystallizable sugar, about seven and a quarter per cent. 2. Uncrystallizable molasses, about seven percent. 3. Acid. 4. Vegetable mucilage, or gum. 5. Coloring matter. 6. Water.

Our object is to separate the sugar and molasses.

The acid and mucilage prevent the sugar from crystallizing.

1. Our first step will be to neutralize the acid in the juice by combining it with an alkali (lime).

2. Our second step will be to remove the mucilage by the addition of liquid albumen (blood, eggs, or milk) to the cold juice, we then apply heat; the albumen, being heated, coagulates, and rising in the form of scum, carries the mucilage with it. This process is called *clarifying*, and should be *twice* repeated at least.

3. Having now got rid of the acid and most of the mucilage, our third step is to remove the *coloring matter*, by filtering the clarified juice through granulated bone black.

But a *peculiar mucilage* still remains, inseparable at a lower heat than about 225° Fahrenheit.

4. Our next step will be to boil the filtered juice to 225° Fahrenheit, and then to add lime water. This mucilage then rises as a scum, and is removed:

We now have left a solution composed of 1. Sugar. 2. Molasses: 3. Water.

5. To crystallize the sugar, we must evaporate the excess of water, by boiling. Most of the sugar will crystallize when the solution grows cold. The uncrystallized part, we drain off as molasses.

These operations require the greatest exactness, for if we do not boil enough, the sugar contained in the solution will not crystallize when cold ; or, if we boil too much, the molasses will become so thick when it cools, as to impair the crystallizing of the sugar, and cannot be separated from it.

But how shall we know when to stop the boiling ?

By the heat of the boiling liquid, as marked by the thermometer.

Pure water boils at 212 degrees of Fahrenheit's thermometer. You cannot make it hotter without changing it to *steam*.

The Sorgho juice, being a solution of about fourteen per cent. of sugar and molasses, &c., in water, becomes three degrees hotter before boiling, and boils at 215° Fahrenheit. As the water evaporates, a greater heat is required to keep the concentrated juice at a boil ; in other words, the juice grows hotter and hotter. When it reaches the heat marked on the thermometer 238° Fahrenheit, there is just enough water left to enable the sugar to separate from the molasses when cold.

6. We now pour the concentrated juice into a mould, a keg, a barrel or other deep vessel, with a plug in the bottom, and allow it to cool.

7. When quite cold (say in twenty-four hours), we remove the plug. The liquid portion, being molasses with a little sugar and water, gradually drains out, leaving the sugar dry in from four to ten days.

It is also important to remember that the juice begins to ferment almost as soon as it leaves the cane, and therefore, should be neutralized, clarified, and boiled *without delay*. A very few hours' delay will spoil it.

A long continued exposure to heat gradually converts crystallizable sugar into uncrystallizable molasses, therefore, the evaporation should be *as rapid as possible*.

A concentrated solution of sugar and molasses is very liable to burn, and should, therefore, be carefully watched, and exposed to a *more and more moderate fire* as the evaporation advances.

The use of a saccharometer is to indicate the relative weight or density of a liquid as compared with water. This density depends upon the amount of sugar, or other heavy substances held in solution. Consequently, the degree of density indicated by the saccharometer is an index of the proportion of sugar, &c., contained in the juice.

It is simply a hollow tube terminating in a bulb, loaded with shot, to keep the bulb down and the tube upright. Floating in pure water, the tube, at the point where it appears above the surface, marks 0. But in proportion as the liquid is heavier, the bulb does not sink so deep, and more of the tube appears above the surface. The density of the Sorgho juice, cold, is about 10° Beaume, so called from Beaume, the inventor.

If your kettles or moulds are of iron, give them two good coats of white paint *inside*, drying each coat thoroughly. This prevents the sugar from being made dark by contact with iron, which will be the case if the slightest acid be present. Before using them, scald them thoroughly *twice*, letting boiling water stand in them until cold, to remove the taste of the paint.

NECESSARY UTENSILS, &c.

1. A thermometer *marking* 250₀ *Fahrenheit*. One without a case, or which can be removed from the case.

2. A saccharometer, or Pese Sirop, scale of Beaume,

You had better get *two of both the above*, to provide against accident.

3. A few sheets of litmus paper.

4. Two kettles of copper, brass, or iron, holding twenty-five gallons each ; one of these may be smaller than the other, but if so, should be as large a diameter, only shallower.

5. Three, or more, large iron sugar moulds, holding twelve gallons each. If you cannot get the sugar moulds, three *long, narrow* twelve gallon kegs will answer.

6. Three five gallon pots of glazed earthen or stone ware, with mouths somewhat smaller than the caps of the sugar moulds. If you use kegs instead of moulds you can use pails instead of pots.

7. A barrel of granulated (not pulverized) bone black, such as is used by sugar refiners.

8. Four ten gallon tubs. (Two water-tight whiskey or cider barrels, sawed across the centre, will answer.)

9. A yard of thick heavy bed ticking.

10. A circular piece of coarse wire gauze, to fit the inside of the sugar mould or keg, three inches above the lower end.

11. A circular piece of half inch board, full of gimlet holes, to fit the inside of the sugar mould or keg, three inches above the lower end.

12: A shallow perforated iron or tin skimmer.

13. A large iron or tin dipper, or ladle.

14. Two simple furnaces, or fire places of brick, upon which to place the two kettles. One larger furnace, with two holes, and one fire place under both kettles, will do, if the kettles are *movable*. But as the labor and delay of lifting them off and on is great, two separate arches are better. These furnaces must have a flue, communicating with a chimney, to create draft, and carry off the smoke.

15. A bushel of quick lime.

16. A gallon of fresh bullock's blood, or twelve dozen of eggs, or twelve quarts of milk. Either will do, but one of the first two is preferable.

PRELIMINARIES.

Having your mill ready, your furnaces built, your kettles and other utensils above described, on the spot,

1. Provide abundant dry fuel, close at hand, and ready for immediate use:

2. Cut and deposit at the mill enough canes for the day's work, say ten canes for each gallon of juice required. Place two tubs (which we will call tubs 1 and 2) at the mill ready to receive the juice.

3. Prepare a bone black filter as follows :—

Take one of the sugar moulds, (which we will call mould No. 1). About three inches from the small end, fit into it the circular piece of half inch board, full of small holes. Upon this, lay the circular piece of wire gauze; over the gauze lay a piece of heavy ticking (or blanket of several thicknesses), laying the edges carefully round the sides of the mould, so as to prevent the bone black from escaping; stop the hole at the small end of the mould, half fill the mould with hot water, then pour in as much bone black as the mould will hold, leaving about three inches of space on top. Set the filter, thus made, upon another of the tubs (which we will call tub No. 3), to serve as a cistern to receive the filtered juice. Or, a filter may be made of a tight keg or barrel, set on end, with a hole in the bottom, stopped with a plug or faucet, and having a wooden second, or false bottom, perforated with gimlet holes, three inches above the first ; cover this with a piece of ticking or blanket, and on that put the bone black, as directed.

4. Prepare some *milk of lime* as follows :—

Put about a gallon of quick lime into a pail, slacken it with water, until it resembles milk in appearance and consistency. Set it aside, and *stir it before using.*

5. Prepare some *lime water* as follows :—

Put a gallon of quick lime into another pail, slacken it, fill up the pail with water, stir it thoroughly, let the lime settle. The clear water will be a saturated solution of lime, and is called lime water. *Do not stir this again,* but use it *clear.*

PROCESS OF MAKING THE SUGAR.

When about twenty gallons of juice are ready, put into one of the kettles, which we will call kettle No. 1, or *the clarifier,* three gills of blood, or the whites of eight eggs, well beaten. If you have neither, two pints of milk will answer, but not so well. Add six tablespoonsful of milk of lime previously prepared, and stirred before using. Add about a gallon of juice, and stir the whole thoroughly together.

Now dip into one of the tubs of unmixed juice a small strip of the blue litmus paper. It will immediately turn red, more or less vivid in proportion to the acidity of the juice. Lay the strip of litmus paper aside, and add to kettle No. 1 about nineteen gallons more of juice; stir the whole. Then dip the strip of reddened litmus paper into the kettle. If it again become blue, the acid is entirely neutralized. If not, continue to stir in milk of lime in small quantities, and to test with the litmus paper, until its original blue color is restored.

Now light a fire under kettle No. 1. As the juice grows hot a thick scum will rise. Do not disturb it, but bring the juice to a boil. To be sure that it does boil, remove a little of the scum with the skimmer, and insert your thermometer. When it marks 215° Fahrenheit, and the scum *begins to roll over,* put out the fire immediately, or remove the kettle. Let it stand ten or fifteen minutes. Then carefully remove the scum with the skimmer into a third pail. Then boil again.

When the saccharometer marks 15° Beaume, in the boiling juice, extinguish the fire, or remove the kettle, and let it cool to 160° Fahrenheit, or cooler. Now stir in six more eggs well beaten, or two gills of blood, or one pint of milk. *Omit the lime.* Again bring it to a boil, again extinguish the fire, or remove the kettle; and, after standing ten minutes, remove the scum as before. Then ladle the clear juice into the bone black filter, (see preliminaries No. 3) having first withdrawn the stopper, allowing the warm water to flow out below, as the juice is poured in above, being careful to keep the filter full of liquid. When the water below begins to run sweet, marking 3_o Beaume, throw away what has previously run out, and receive the remainder in tub No. 3.

We are now ready to continue evaporation, and it will be better to do so in smaller quantities, as in a shallower mass the concentration will be more rapid. Therefore, when about ten gallons have passed through the filter into tub 3, ladle into kettle No. 2, which now first comes into use, and which we will call the *Evaporator.* Boil to 225° Fahrenheit. Then put in a gill of clear lime water (see preliminaries No. 5.) If a dirty white scum arise skim it off, and continue to add a little more lime water every few minutes until no scum rises. Continue to boil to 238° Fahrenheit. If it boil over, put in a piece of butter the size of a walnut; then remove the kettle, or put out the fire, and pour into a tub which we will call No. 4.

By this time ten gallons more will have passed through the filter. Ladle it into kettle No. 2, which we have just emptied, boil to 225_o Fahrenheit, clarify with lime water as before, boil to 238° Fahrenheit, and add it to the contents of tub No. 4, stirring the two together.

Previously, however, as soon as kettle No. 1 has been emptied upon the bone black filter, put into kettle No. 1 milk of lime and eggs, (or blood, or milk) as before, and neutralize and clarify twenty gallons more of fresh juice from the mill, which has been grinding without interruption. This second charge of kettle No. 1 should be neutralized, tested with litmus paper, heated to 215° Fahrenheit, cooled, skimmed, boiled to 15° Beaume, cooled again, a second time clarified with eggs, skimmed again, and passed through the filter; all this being done simultaneously with the filtering and evaporation of the first charge of kettle No. 1. It will then be put, in its turn, into kettle No. 2, now again empty, ten gallons at a time, boiled to 225_o Fahrenheit, clarified a third time with lime water, skimmed, evaporated to 238° Fahrenheit, and added to the contents of tub No. 4.

While the second charge of kettle No. 1 is passing through the filter and kettle No. 2, a third charge of twenty gallons of fresh juice will be neutralized and clarified in kettle No. 1.

C

While the third charge from kettle No. 1 is passing through the filter, and kettle No. 2, a fourth charge of twenty gallons of fresh juice will be neutralized and clarified in kettle No. 1, to follow the others, when boiled down to 238° Fahrenheit, into tub No. 4.

When as much juice as can be boiled the same day has been expressed, *stop the mill.*

Eighty gallons of juice clarified and boiled down to 238° Fahrenheit will be reduced to something over twelve gallons, or enough to fill one of the sugar moulds.

When the day's boiling is completed, put the contents of tub No. 4 into a sugar mould or keg, having previously plugged the hole. Set it in a warm place, in no case colder than 60° Fahrenheit; if 70° or 80°, so much the better. This completes the day's work.

When cold, the next day, it will be a solid mass of crystallized sugar. Then withdraw the stopper, set the mould on an earthen pot or pail ; in from four to seven days the molasses will have ceased to drain out; then turn over the mould upon a clean board or table, strike the rim smartly once or twice, and the sugar will slide from the mould in a solid mass. Break it up with a shovel, and it is fit for use. The contents of this mould should be from forty to fifty pounds of dry, yellow sugar, and about four gallons of excellent molasses will have dripped from it into the jar.

If preferred, the sugar making may here terminate; but, as the purifying power of the bone black filter is not yet exhausted, and as the whole labor and expense of preparation have been already incurred, it will be best to continue at least a second and third day.

Second Day.—The process will be in all respects a repetition of the first day's work, and the result will be to fill an additional sugar mould or keg.

Third Day.—The process will be a repetition of the above ; but the filter being now exhausted, after the third day, it will be necessary to change the bone black. Before emptying the filter, or stopping the third day's work, however, pass cold water through the filter, which, so long as it runs sweet enough to mark 3° Beaume, is to be added to the juice of the upper joints, of which we are about to speak.

MOLASSES.

At the close of the sugar making, pass through the mill the upper joints of the canes, previously laid aside. Add to the juice the liquid portion of the scum in third pail, together with the washings of the filter, of tub No. 4, and of other utensils. Neutralize the acid with milk of lime, and test with litmus paper as before. Clarify twice with eggs, (or blood, or milk) but omit, if preferred, the filtering through bone black. Boil finally only to 228° Fahrenheit, instead of 238° as for sugar.

The product, when cool, will be about eighteen gallons of excellent syrup. From three days' work, of two hundred and forty gallons of juice —from say two thousand canes—there should be a total product of about one hundred and twenty-five to one hundred and fifty pounds of sugar, and twenty-seven gallons molasses.

This operation being on a very small scale, is carried on under great disadvantages. The same labor on a larger scale would produce much greater results. The process and routine here given will answer for larger operations. It would be better, however, especially if the quantity is increased, to have the second or evaporating kettle of greater length and breadth, and as shallow as possible to expedite the evaporation. A larger and longer bone black filter will also be needed.

Either sugar or molasses of good quality, but of darker color, may be made by the above process, omitting the bone black. If it be desired to make syrup only, stop the boiling at 228° Fahrenheit.

If white sugar is desired, the following additional process will be necessary. On the third day after the sugar has been put into the moulds, the greater part of the molasses having drained from it, scrape off with a knife, the crust on top of the sugar, leaving a smooth granulated surface, hollowing a little to the centre. Moisten the scrapings with cold water into a thin paste, and replace them on the sugar. Next day dissolve enough refined sugar, the whiter the better, in six quarts of water, to make a solution marking, when boiling hot, 32° Beaume. Pour one inch in depth of this solution, cold, on top of the sugar. On each of the two following days, put on a similar quantity. After the sugar ceases to drain, knock out the loaf; the upper portion will be white, the lower part light yellow. Divide the loaf and crush each portion separately.

If by any mistake, or carelessness, by burning or overboiling, or by the immaturity of the canes, the molasses should not begin to drain from the mould on the second or third day, run an awl, a large nail or other sharp iron instrument, into the hole at the foot of the mould some two or three inches, and then withdraw it. If, after ten days longer in the warmest place you have, it still fails to run, put the contents into a kettle, add a little water, heat it to 228° Fahrenheit, and it will make good syrup.

It is proper to state that Mr. Lovering's experiments, on which he has based the above practical instructions, have been made on a sufficiently extensive scale to justify their being taken as a basis for calculating general results. From the various and necessarily somewhat conflicting statements of different experimenters, I estimate that we shall be safe in assuming that an acre of Sorgho, cultivated in the manner I have described, and crushed with a tolerably efficient mill, will yield at least 1800 gallons of juice, containing from 10 to 12 per cent. of sugar and molasses, which, if successfully treated according to Mr. Lovering's process, will be converted into about 1200 lbs. of good sugar, equal to what is called the *Clayed Muscovado*, and 80 gallons of molasses. Again I would remind you that the season in which the experiments furnishing the data for this estimate were made was remarkably unfavorable, and that I have purposely selected the most moderate statements of results ; consequently I believe there is little room to fear disappointment in attaining at least the yield I have specified.*

SYRUP.

I have hitherto, in these remarks, purposely confined your attention to the cultivation of this crop, with a view exclusively to the manufacture of sugar from its product. This method I have followed partly to simplify my own task in the treatment of the subject, but mainly on the principle of aiming at the highest and most valuable results in the first instance. But there are many other highly important economic uses to which this plant may be converted, as has been proved by ample experience. I refer, in the first place, to Syrup, an article which is daily coming more into demand in this country.

Whatever difference of opinion may have existed, previously to Mr. Lovering's successful experiments, as to the prospects of obtaining crystalized sugar from the juice of the Sorgho, it has been unanimously admitted, since its first introduction, to be capable of yielding an abundant supply of the best quality of Syrup, and thus becoming a source of considerable national wealth.

One very important advantage incident to this method of disposing of the crop, is that it is not essential (although certainly preferable) that the canes be fully ripe ; therefore, should the season be unpropitious, or the cultivation, from whatever cause, unsuccessful in producing the degree of

---

* Mr. Lovering states that by strict attention to the rules he has laid down, it is as easy to make good sugar from the Chinese Sugar Cane as to make a pot of good mush, or a kettle of good apple jelly.

maturity necessary for the production of crystalized sugar, the crop may be turned to good account in making syrup. The method is as follows : The kettles may be such as described for the sugar-making process ; the juice should be put into them immediately after being pressed out, and at once put on the fires, which should be so arranged that they may be under perfect control. The juice should first be heated slowly, and allowed to simmer until a thick green scum rises to the surface and forms into puffs seeming ready to crack. This scum, when fully developed, should be skimmed off very carefully. The heat may now be raised to boiling point, and the juice kept in an active state of ebullition until the bulk is reduced one-half. Great care must be taken to avoid scorching, and the skimming should be continued throughout the process until the syrup thickens and hangs in flakes from the ladle, when it is ready. It is desirable (though not indispensable) to use an instrument to ascertain the proper degree of concentration, as, if not boiled down sufficiently, the syrup is liable to ferment. Should the slightly acid taste which it will have be objectionable, it may be removed by adding a little quicklime or soda after the scum has been removed ; but the quantity should not exceed one teaspoonful to five gallons of juice.

An acre of the canes, even with very imperfect apparatus, has been proved capable of producing from 300 to 400 gallons of syrup of a quality not to be surpassed by any in the market. With the addition of a small per centage of honey, it is said to be scarcely distinguishable from true honey. It is almost superfluous to remark, that both in sugar and syrup making the strictest cleanliness, attention and method must be observed at every stage.

Should this new branch of domestic industry tend to promote these secondary virtues in Canada, this may rank as not the least important of the benefits attending its introduction

ALCOHOL

Is another of the products which may be obtained in great perfection and to great advantage from the Sorgho plant ; and whatever may be our opinions as to its indiscriminate use as a beverage, it is certain that it will continue to be an article of large and general consumpt in various forms. If it can be shewn that the Chinese Sugar Cane will yield a supply of alcohol as economically as the cereals from which it is now chiefly derived, these will advantageously be returned to their more legitimate channels of consumption. I do not mean to enter into the details of the manufacture, but merely to state the probable results.

It is well known that in order to produce the vinous or alcoholic fermentation in a fluid, it is first necessary that it should be sweet, and this sweetness, where naturally wanting, as in grain, must be induced by artificial means. The juice of the sorgho is in precisely the most suitable state for producing, with very slight artificial aid, the desired condition. Canes that have been damaged by prostration by the wind, or any other cause, or that have not come to maturity, together with the scum and refuse from sugar or syrup making, are perfectly suitable for adding to the raw material of the alcohol manufacture; which, however, I presume would scarcely be attempted by individual farmers on the same limited scale as the syrup making.

It has been ascertained by careful experiment that 22 gallons of juice, at the ordinary density, will yield 1¾ gallon of alcohol, at 90 per cent. or 40 over proof. Now, supposing an acre of sorgho to yield only 1500 gallons of juice, this would be equivalent to 214 gallons of proof spirits of a purer and more wholesome quality than most of the deleterious trash now palmed off upon the public.

OTHER PRODUCTS.

In addition to the foregoing, there are other products which may be economically derived from this interesting plant. These, though all tending materially to enhance its value and 'stimulate to its introduction amongst us, I must on the present occasion content myself with merely enumerating. The first of these is *Vinegar*, said to be of excellent quality and capable of being produced at the rate of 1200 to 1500 gallons per acre. *Beer*, a very wholesome and agreeable beverage, resembling cider, and which is produced with very little trouble. *Starch*, of which the seeds yield 45 per cent. of their weight, and of a quality well worthy the attention of manufacturers of this article. *Dye Stuffs*, much esteemed in France, are derived from the hulls of the seeds, varying from a light buff to a very deep purple. *Paper* has been manufactured from the pulpy stalks, naturally sized, strong and remarkably adapted to resist moisture.

FORAGE.

Last, but not least important of all the beneficial uses to which these grasses may be applied, is as a fodder crop; in fact, even if applicable to no other purpose, they would be invaluable for this alone. In this country, owing to the frequent failures of the hay crop, and other circumstances rendering the supplies of forage precarious, too little attention is bestowed on that most important department of farming industry, the rearing of stock. The leaves and stalks of the Sorgho, whether as green fodder or dry, are devoured with avidity by cattle and horses ; and as it is a well-known fact that sugar contains more nourishment than almost any other vegetable product, the result of using such food cannot fail to put and preserve the animals in good condition. Accordingly, it has been ascertained that milch cows fed with it have speedily shown a marked improvement both in the quantity and quality of the milk which they produce. Horses can be fed on the green fodder, and, with the addition of a little hay, kept in good working condition without the use of oats. The seeds, of which the yield is from 25 to 50 bushels per acre, may be fed to horses instead of oats, and for fattening pigs and poultry are un-equalled, although they are said to tinge the bones of animals fed with them.

In cultivating for its forage exclusively, the seeds should be sown in drills two feet apart, letting fall from 15 to 20 seeds to the foot. If sown broadcast, it will require about one-and-a-half bushel of seed to an acre. In using as green fodder, the first cutting (as there will be at least two, and perhaps three, in the season) may be made when the plants are three or four feet high, or at the time when, in this part of the country, grass is scarce, owing to the hay harvest. After attaining a certain stage of growth, the sorgho seems to be comparatively unaffected by continued drouths. As green fodder it will yield about 20 tons to an acre.

For a dry winter crop, to quote from Mr. Olcott, "it should be cut in the morning, when the dew is off the plants, and suffered to lie on the ground and become well dried before being bound up. The bundles should be small, and before stacking or putting into the barn, should be set up in groups in the field to cause further drying. The stack should, of course, be built on rails or other convenient poles, to allow of a circulation of air beneath ; and to carry out this requisition to a greater extent, it is well to build the stack round rails set up on end and leaning inward to-wards the centre ; by which plan the interior of the stack is in direct contact with the atmosphere, and thus heating will not be so liable to oc-cur. The extra trouble of curing is amply repaid by the increased pro-duct as compared with hay ; but with every precaution it may occur, that an inexperienced person will not be liable to save his crop in good condi-tion on a first trial." The yield of dried forage per acre will be from 6 to 10 tons ; that of hay rarely exceeding $1\frac{3}{4}$ ton. Stalks which are dry be-fore cutting, as also crushed canes, should on no account be fed to cattle.

THE IMPHEE, OR AFRICAN SUGAR CANE.

Having treated so fully of the Sorgho, I shall not trespass upon your patience by giving any detailed account of the Imphee, or African Sugar Cane; and this is the less necessary, seeing it is only another variety of the same plant, and the nature of its products, and manner of cultivation and treatment are nearly identical. I shall merely state very briefly wherein the principal points of difference consist.

The Imphee is a native of South Africa, and was introduced into Europe and America by Mr. Leonard Wray, a most intelligent Planter and Sugar Refiner. Mr. Wray has discovered no less than fifteen different varieties of the plant, each possessing distinctive qualities, chiefly referring to the periods of coming to maturity. Three of these, the Nee-a-za-na, the Boom-vwa-na, and the Oom si-a-na, he considers to be peculiarly adapted for Northern growth—reaching perfection in little more than three months from the time of sowing.

The cultivation of the African Sugar Cane in America has not yet been subjected to the test of experience to such an extent as that of the Chinese variety; but if the anticipations formed by Mr. Wray of its adaptation to northerly climates should be verified, there can be little doubt that its rapidity of growth and ripening, combined with its other superior qualities, will cause it to be preferred in this country to the Sorgho, which takes from four to five months to ripen. This is a point of so much importance to be ascertained in the outset, that it is to be hoped experiments will be tried this season in Canada with some of the above-named varieties of the Imphee, as well as with the Sorgho.

In judging of the ripeness of the Imphee seed the cultivator must not be misguided by any previous experience or any instructions referring to the Chinese cane; for while, in the latter case, he would wait for the seeds turning black before he would feel authorized in harvesting his crop, on the other hand the seeds of some varieties of the Imphee, when fully ripe, are of a light buff color, and the only reliable test, in that case, will be their plumpness and hardness.

The juice of the Imphee is naturally more limpid, less mucilaginous, and more free from extractive matter, and therefore more easy to defecate and more ready to crystalize than that of the Sorgho. These qualities should give it a great advantage in regard to the making of sugar. The juice seems also to be more copious and richer, but this may perhaps be attributed to its having as yet been tried only in southerly latitudes. The stalks are thicker and the seed-heads lighter than those of the Sorgho, which will render them not so readily prostrated by high winds; an accident against which every precaution should be taken, although even should it occur, the crop, whether of Sorghee or Imphee, is by no means necessarily ruined. Such are the chief points of difference of the two plants, and on all these accounts, provided the African variety can be acclimated in this country, it will probably be preferable to the other.

COST OF PRODUCTION.

It will obviously be impossible to give anything approaching to an exact estimate of the cost of producing any of the articles which these plants are capable of yielding; even if the fact of their successful cultivation in this country were fully established, instead of being only as yet highly probable, the diversity in the value of land and in the cost of different methods of operating will modify the ultimate cost greatly. I shall, however, from such data as I have been able to ascertain, attempt an approximation, premising that as I have selected the most moderate and reliable statements as to the yield of the crops, I shall now set down the value of the land and apparatus, and the labor in working, at a figure which, if an error, will be on the safe side.

FOR SUGAR.

Value of an acre of land, say $60 } $160, Ten per cent. rent....$16.00
Say for sugar mill.........$100 }
Seed, eight lbs. at 25 cents,................................. 2.00
Cultivation and harvesting................................. 10.00
Labor at mill and boiling, &c.............................. 20.00
Interest on cost of utensils, bone black filter, &c.............. 8.00

Cost to convert produce of an acre into sugar.................$56.00

This sum divided by 1200 lbs.—say the yield of sugar per acre—gives about 4¾ cents as the cost of a pound of sugar—the selling price at present being about double. In this estimate no account is taken of the value of molasses, of which there will be 80 gallons; and this, at the present selling price, 38 cents, should be worth over $30.

SYRUP.

Cost of producing, including rent of land, use of mill and utensils, &c.—say..$50.00
Produce of syrup per acre—say 300 gallons; therefore cost of producing one gallon, 16 cents—the present price being 50 cents.

ALCOHOL.

Cost of producing syrup $40.00
Add cost of fermenting and distilling (ample allowance) 20.00

Cost to convert produce of an acre into alcohol.............. $60.00

This sum divided by 214—the number of gallons of proof spirits readily obtainable from an acre of sorgho—gives 28 cents as the cost of a gallon, the market price being at present about 40 cents.

D

Again, if we compare the price of wheat and the cost of its production with those of sorgho sugar, we shall find the result equally favorable to the latter.

Value of an acre of land—say as before $60
Proportion of value of stock and utensils—say $20

Interest, at 10 per cent., on........................ $80 .... $8.00
      Cost of cultivating an acre of wheat—say $7.00

Cost to produce 20 bushels of wheat (a high average per acre)... $15.00
Therefore—cost of a bushel of wheat 00.75
Price with which farmers are content in ordinary times......... 1.00
    or 25 per cent.—a fair and legitimate working profit.
Cost to produce one pound of sugar, as before—say............4¾ cents.
Market price   do.   do. 9   "
Difference 4¼ cents, or nearly 100 per cent. profit on the transaction.

From the above rough estimates, it appears very clearly that the manufacture of syrup from these juices is, in the meantime, much the most profitable, as it will also, on other accounts, probably prove the most desirable mode of disposing of them.

STATISTICS OF THE SUGAR TRADE.

As bearing directly on the subject before us, I shall now introduce to your notice a few facts derived from official, and otherwise trustworthy sources, in regard to the consumption of Sugar and Syrups in Canada. It is on the eloquence of facts and figures simply that I rely for whatever effect this discourse may produce upon your minds ; and the statements I have now to offer will illustrate the magnitude and importance of the interests at stake more forcibly than any other species of argument.

In 1851, the quantity of Sugar imported into Canada was 20,175,046 pounds, amounting in value to $925,604 ; the total population, according to the census taken in that year, being 1,842,265. These figures indicate a consumption of about eleven pounds of Sugar annually per head, exclusive of Maple Sugar.

In 1857, the importations were 29,227,000 pounds, exclusive of that imported by Messrs. Redpath for manufacture in the Province, say, 4,000,000 pounds, amounting in the aggregate to 33,227,000 pounds, value $2,128,745. The estimated population for that year was 2,571,437, being at the rate of about thirteen pounds per head, exclusive of Maple Sugar ; thus verifying the remark I made at the outset with regard to the increasing demand for this article. The estimated annual consumption per head of the population in Great Britain is twenty-four pounds, and in the United States thirty pounds.

The importation of Molasses and Syrup in 1853 was 1,406,525 gallons ; value $213,480; in 1857 (including that manufactured by Messrs. Redpath) it was 1,540,073 gallons, valued at $400,000 ; the disproportion between the relative quantities and prices in these years respectively being due to the increasing demand for a higher grade or better quality of the article, as well as to the rise in price. At the rate of 300 gallons produce of Syrup to the acre, it would require a breadth of about 6000 acres of the Sorgho crop, exclusively devoted to the Syrup manufacture, to supply the present demand. The field of commercial enterprise thus opened up seems well worthy the immediate attention of enterprising capitalists.

It would be premature to speak in the same terms with regard to the manufacture of Sugar on an extensive scale ; but it may be relied on as an undoubted fact, that whatever measure of success or good results may be achieved by the manufacture on a small scale, after the process I have described, would be augmented by at least twenty per cent. in quantity, and indefinitely in quality, in the event of its being taken up as a separate branch of business, and with all proper appliances. The beet-root contains only ten per cent of saccharine matter ; yet France by bringing her unbounded scientific resources to bear upon it, has been enabled to produce 150,000,000 pounds of sugar from that root ; a quantity equal to one half of what is consumed by her entire population of 30,000,000. By applying the same skill, energy and judgment in the cultivation and utilization of the new Sugar Plants, which contain from thirteen to sixteen per cent. I shall not surely be condemned as an enthusiast for expressing the hope and expectation of similar great results.

While the demand for sugar is, as I have shown, increasing from year to year, the supplies from the ordinary sources are continually undergoing reduction. In the British West Indies (with some exceptions) the liberated negroes find employment more congenial to their tastes than the drudgery of the cane field and sugar-mill. In France, the beet root has of late years been to a considerable extent withdrawn from the manufacture of sugar to that of alcohol. In Louisiana the planters have latterly found it more profitable to grow cotton than sugar ; and generally throughout the sugar-producing countries, the soils are exhausted, and the canes deteriorated from being propagated exclusively from slips or cuttings. In all these circumstances it is to be hoped, as there is also good grounds for believing, that whether experience will prove the possibility of producing sugar in Canada profitably and economically, or otherwise, yet at all events the area of the sugar-producing regions will be greatly extended by the introduction of these plants.

In again recommending their immediate and extensive introduction, I should be sorry to be understood as detracting from the importance or discouraging the cultivation of Wheat and Corn. It is undoubtedly on these crops that our commercial prosperity has hitherto mainly depended, and must continue to depend. The soil and climate of Western Canada are peculiarly well adapted for their growth, and they must ever be regarded as the staple, and as it were, the legitimate products of the country, as Sugar, Cotton and Rice are of the more Southerly latitudes. However discouraging or depressing may be the prospects of the wheat trade, from the experience of the past two years, the circumstances which have produced these reverses must be regarded as temporary and remediable. Still, however, there is "ample room and verge enough" both in the extent and natural capabilities of the Province itself, and in the enterprise and energy of its inhabitants, for the development of this new branch of agricultural industry. In thus acting as pioneer, and endeavoring to remove some of the obstructions lying in the path, I shall be happy if my humble efforts should have the effect of leading to the cultivation of the new Sugar Plants on an adequate scale, and of inspiring intending cultivators with that degree of hope and confidence which is the best earnest of a successful issue.

APPENDIX.

Since writing the foregoing Essay, I have seen the Report for 1858 of the United States Agricultural Society upon the subject of which it treats; and I gladly avail myself of this opportunity of diffusing the valuable information it contains.

REPORT OF THE UNITED STATES AGRICULTURAL SOCIETY.

Conformably to the resolutions adopted by the United States Agricultural Society, held at the city of Washington in January, 1857, the committee appointed to investigate and experiment upon the *Sorgho sucre*, or Chinese Sugar-cane, with the view of determining its value for the purposes of syrup and sugar-making, soiling cattle, use of the seed for feeding stock, for bread-making, and for the manufacture of paper, and alcoholic liquors, beg leave to report as follows :—

Agreeably to the requirements, there was imported from France sufficient sorgho seed to plant 100 acres of land. This seed was placed in the hands of a number of individuals in different sections of the country, who cultivated it under various conditions of soil, climate, &c. From the results of their experiments, in ninety localities, between New Brunswick, in the British dominions, and Mexico on the one hand, and between Florida and Washington Territory on the other; though contradictory or conflicting with each other in some instances, the committee arrived at the following conclusions :

1. The soil and geographical range of the Chinese Sugar-cane correspond nearly with those of Indian corn, and it thrives with great luxuriance in rich bottom lands, or in moist loamy soils, well manured. It will also produce a fair crop on dry, sandy, or gravelly soils too poor to give a remunerative crop of other plants. On the latter class of soils, however, it proved more profitable to the cultivator where there had been applied a moderate quantity of bone-dust, wood-ashes, poudrette, phosphated guano, gypsum, or super-phosphate of lime.

2. This plant endures cold much better than corn, and resists without injury the ordinary autumnal frosts. It will also withstand excessive drought. In favorable seasons, when planted early in May, it will ripen its seeds in September, if the soil be dry and warm, in many parts of the extreme Northern and New England States, and in October in the Middle and Southern States, when planted as late as the 20th of June. At the extreme South, it may be planted successively from January into July.

3. The cost and culture of this plant does not differ essentially from that of Indian corn. The seeds require to be planted at different distances apart, according to the strength of the soil. On light, moderately rich land, it succeeded best when sown in rows or drills, three feet apart, with the plants a foot asunder along the drills, or in hills with a corresponding number of stalks to each; but on richer land, it has been found

preferable to plant the hills four or five feet asunder. If cultivated exclusively for soiling or dry fodder, the seed may be sown broad-cast or in drills, and treated in the same manner as Indian corn when grown for that use.

4. The height of the plant when fully grown varies from 6 to 18 feet, according to the locality and the condition of the soil ; the stalks ranging from half an inch to two inches in diameter. The weight of the entire crop to an acre, when green, varies from 10 to 40 tons. The amount of seed to the acre is reported to range from 16 to 50 bushels.

5. During the earlier stages of the growth of this plant, say for the first six or eight weeks, it makes but little progress, except in penetrating the ground with its roots, which occasioned so great disappointment in some cultivators that they exterminated it from their fields, and replanted for other crops. From the natural tendency of the genus to which it belongs to sport or run into varieties, many persons have come to wrong conclusions with a belief that the seed was impure or mixed. The period of growth varied from ninety to one hundred and twenty days ; the seeds often ripen unequally in the same field.

6. The yield of juice in weight of well-trimmed stalks was about 50 per cent. The number of gallons of juice required to make a gallon of syrup varied from 5 to 10, according to the locality, the nature of the soil on which it was produced, and the succulent condition or maturity of the canes. In the Province of New Brunswick it required 10 to 1 ; in the rich bottom lands of Indiana and Illinois about 7 to 1 ; and in light lands in Maryland and Virginia, 5 gallons to 1 of syrup. The yield of syrup per acre varied from 150 to 400 gallons. The amount of pure alcohol produced by the juice ranged from 5 to 9 per cent. In cases where the plant was well matured and grew upon a warm, light soil, the juice yielded from 13 to 16 per cent. of dry saccharine matter ; from 9 to 11 per cent. of which was well-defined crystallized cane-sugar, and the remainder, uncrystallizable matter, or glucose ; but that taken from stalks obtained on rich low-lands, luxuriant in their growth, yielded considerably less.

7. A palatable bread was made from the flour ground from the seeds of this plant, of a pinkish color, caused by the remnants of the pellicles, or hulls, of the seeds.

8. By accounts from all parts of the country, this plant is universally admitted to be a wholesome, nutritious, and economical food for animals ; all parts of it being greedily devoured, in a green or dried state, by horses, cattle, sheep, poultry, and swine, without injurious effects ; the two latter fattening upon it equally as well as upon corn.

9. Paper of various qualities has been manufactured from the fibrous parts of the stalk, some of which appear to be peculiarly fitted for special use, such as bank notes, wrapping paper, &c.

From the above summary, the committee are of opinion that the Sorgho possesses qualities which commend it to the especial attention of the agriculturists of all parts of the country, as the preceding facts have demonstrated that it is well suited to our national economy, and supplies what has long been a great desideratum.

I have been favored by Dr. Hurlburt with the following interesting statements relative to the growth of Indian Corn and the Sugar Cane; and which, as they bear directly on the subject now treated of, and corroborate the views expressed in this Essay, I have much pleasure in appending to it :—

CLIMATOLOGICAL RANGE OF INDIAN CORN.

The Sugar Cane proper being a tropical plant, and the Indian Corn being indigenous to the warmer latitudes of America, of course grow more readily in proportion as we approach the Equator. The Cane has ripened as far North as the 35th parallel on the Mississippi. Indian Corn is the successor of the Cane in the North, and has ripened as high as lat. 54o on the Saskatchewan. It is peculiarly elastic in its adaptation to climates, requiring, however, in all cases a high temperature during the three summer months, say about 65o mean temperature, with one month as high as 67o. Thus in the Lower Mississippi, seven or eight months may intervene from the planting to the ripening ; whereas on the Red River at lat. 50o, one variety matures in two and a half months. Commencing at the Atlantic coast, the Northern limits of this cereal may be roughly traced as running through some parts of the Valley of St. John in New Brunswick, reappearing on the Saguenay, thence running a little North of Quebec and high up the Ottawa, and embracing nearly all the settled parts of Upper Canada. The high lands, both North and South of Lake Superior, have too low a temperature, but it ripens well again in the valleys of the Red, Assiniboine and Saskatchewan Rivers as high as lat. 54o.

Thus if the Sorgho will grow and ripen, as seems probable, under the same conditions of climate as the Indian Corn, there is a vast area adapted to it even in British North America. Of course, there are many localities within these limits where the temperature is too low for Indian Corn, as also in the New England States and New York. In New England, an altitude exceeding one thousand feet above the level of the sea ; as also in New York a large area North of Albany and Utica; and in the Southern parts of the State, on the borders of Pennsylvania,—are unfavorable.

The growth of Indian Corn has, within a century, extended from the sub-tropical regions to lat. 54o. The Sugar Cane proper now matures much further North than its native regions. We may reasonably expect the Sorgho to follow the same law, and adapt itself to the shorter summers of high latitudes, requiring however the one condition of a high temperature during the summer months.

J. HURLBURT.

I have also much pleasure in adding the following extract of a letter from a highly intelligent friend residing in our immediate neighbourhood, who has long been impressed with the importance of this subject :—

The first seed sown in this quarter, (Beamsville) was obtained from Mr. Judd, Publisher of the *American Agriculturist*, in 1857. He sent to each subscriber a paper containing a small quantity. It was labelled *Chinese*, not African. It ripened very well, and yielded the seed of many considerable patches last year ; but many farmers, anxious to test it on a larger scale, sent to New York last Spring for larger parcels of seed, and planted from one-eighth to one fourth acre. I know of no larger patch planted hereabout. The best soil for it is a rich, sandy loam. Indeed, as regards *soil, time and mode of planting and cultivation*, it requires the same treatment as Indian Corn ; but Mr. Isaac Hann, who cultivated it very successfully, says instead of planting in hills eighteen inches apart, he purposes this year to plant in *rows*, about six inches apart in the row; but the rows, as the hills were, about two and a half feet apart. It grew to an average height of twelve feet, stalks about three inches in circumference, and ripened in three to four months. He got Mr. Harris, of the Clinton Foundry here, to construct a mill for crushing the stalks— a simple adaptation of three cylinders—driven by this ordinary horse power. With this he crushed his own, and lots for several neighbours. From one-fourth of an acre he got about three hundred and fifty gallons of sap, which yielded ninety gallons of syrup. He has promised to bring me a bottle of the syrup to see and taste it. If he does, I shall endeavor to send it to you. It sells readily at 50 cents per gallon ; indeed, he got 75 cents for some. He treated the sap about the same way as the maple sap is treated, but did not succeed in making sugar. The same process by which maple sugar is made, does not suffice for this. It is still a desideratum. I took a bottle of syrup, made by Mr. Russ, to the Provincial Fair last year, but it was not liked. It had a vegetable taste ; it was made from the sap before being quite ripe. I believe the only way to avoid that peculiar taste is to have the Cane well ripened, and even get a touch of frost.

J. B. OSBORNE.

BEAMSVILLE, 19th April, 1859.

Last season also a crop of the Chinese Sugar Cane flourished vigorously, and came to maturity at Woodstock, C.W., between 700 and 800 feet above the level of Lake Ontario, or upwards of 1000 feet above the level of the sea, and probably about the highest arable land in Canada West.